Little Fella

Superbuddy

by
Sarah McConnell

ORCHARD BOOKS

For Ian, with love

ORCHARD BOOKS
96 Leonard Street, London EC2A 4XD
Orchard Books Australia
32/45-51 Huntley Street, Alexandria, NSW 2015
HB ISBN 1 84121 619 4
PB ISBN 1 84362 023 5
First published in Great Britain in 2002
First paperback publication in 2003
Text and Illustrations © Sarah McConnell 2002
The right of Sarah McConnell to be identified as the author and
illustrator of this Work has been asserted by her
in accordance with the Copyright, Designs and Patents Act, 1988.
A CIP catalogue record for this book is available from the British Library.
1 3 5 7 9 10 8 6 4 2 (hardback)
1 3 5 7 9 10 8 6 4 2 (paperback)
Printed in Dubai

Little Fella's name is Joe but everyone calls him Little Fella because he's not very big.

Little Fella loves being a superhero. Every day he bounces out of his bed,

BOUNCE!

squeezes into his superhero suit,

SQUEEZE!

One morning after gulping down an extremely large bowl of superflakes, Little Fella jumped into his supercart and,

WHEE!

off he went to the playground with Big Sister.

Two big boys were playing basketball. It looked like fun.

"Can I play?" asked Little Fella.

"You must be joking," said one boy.

"You're too short," said the other.

And just to prove it, they threw the ball high over Little Fella's head.

Boing!

Boing!

BOING!

"Ouch!"

"Are you OK?" said Little Fella.

"No," sniffed a girl, rubbing her head. "Pogo's gone."

"Who's Pogo?" asked Little Fella. "She's my favourite squashy toy," said the girl, "and I've lost her somewhere in the playground."

"That sounds like
a job for a superhero,"
said Little Fella, swirling
his cape and stamping his
big lace-up boots.

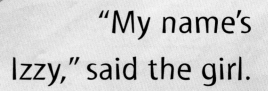

"Is Pogo a teddy bear?" asked Little Fella.

"No!" said Izzy. "A duck?"

"No!" said Izzy. "A rabbit?"

"Nooo!" said Izzy.

"Pogo's blue and lumpy."

"Little Fella Superhero to the rescue," said Little Fella. "Let's find Pogo."

Little Fella and Izzy pushed through the thickest jungle.

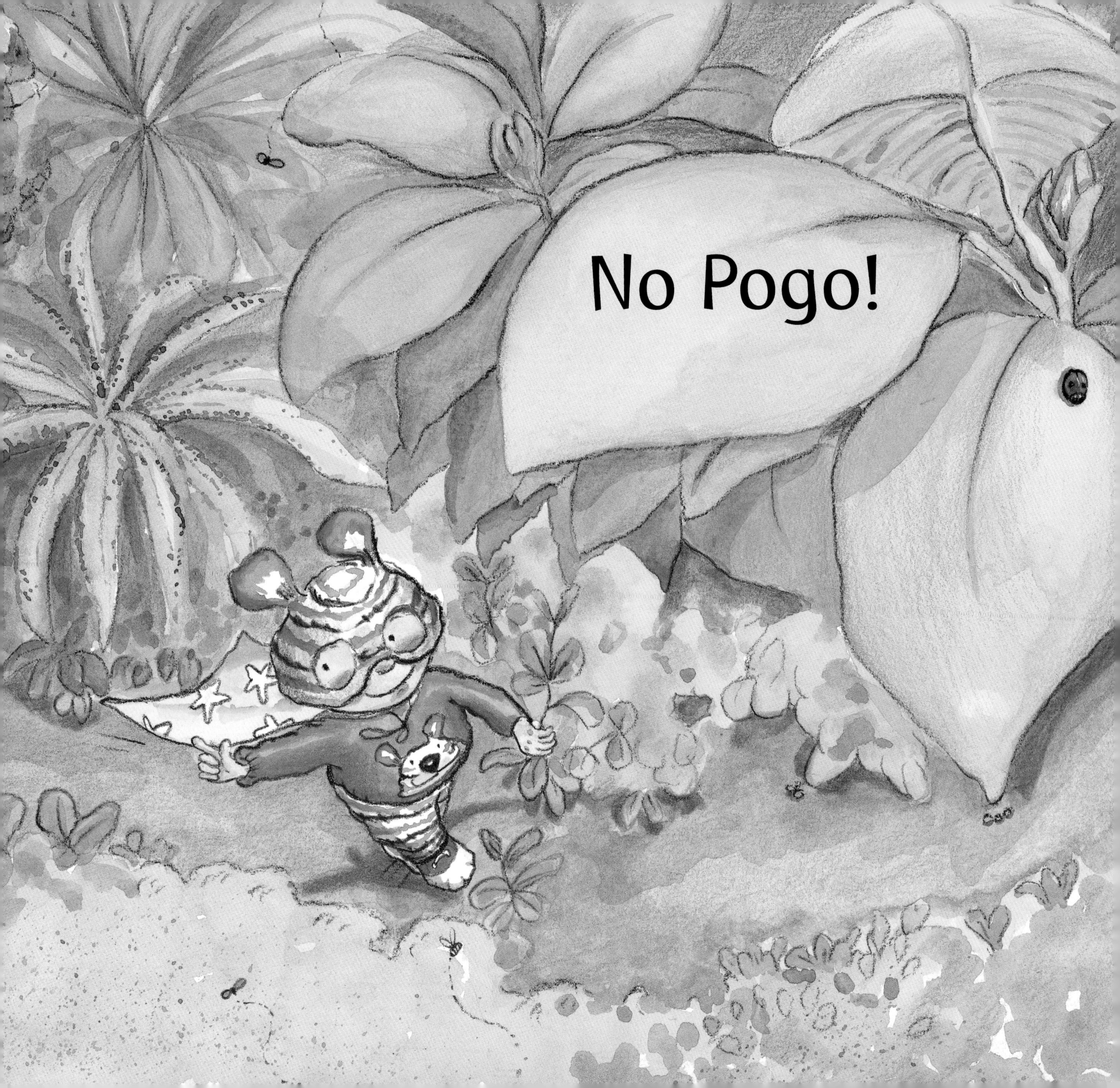

No Pogo!

Little Fella and Izzy
dived to the bottom of
the deep blue sea.

No Pogo!

Little Fella and Izzy climbed
to the top of the highest mountain.

Still no Pogo!

But then ...

"Look!" shouted Izzy. "There's Pogo!"
On the other side of the fence,
the two big boys were using
poor Pogo as a basketball,
throwing her up and
down through the hoop.

"Quickly, we've got to save her!"
said Little Fella, and he whispered
in Izzy's ear.

Little Fella and Izzy

t i p t o e d

up to the wall . . .

creeping **closer**
and **closer** ...

Pogo shot straight out of
the boys' hands and into the air.
She spun round and round,
twisting and turning until …

plop!

"Aha," said Little Fella, giggling.
"So that's what a Pogo
looks like!"
"Quick!" said Izzy.
"We've got to go."

"Which way?" said Little Fella.

"This way," said Izzy.

And in a flash they were off . . .

up the mountain,

across
the sea,

through
the jungle . . .

and right back to where Izzy's mum and Little Fella's big sister were waiting.

"That was fun," said Izzy.
"Does this mean we're friends?"
"We're not just friends!"
said Little Fella, rummaging
in his supercart ...

"We're Superbuddies!"